The Three Little Pigs

and other bedtime stories

Contents

ARCTURUS

The Three Little Pigs

Once upon a time,
there were three little pigs
who lived with their mother.

The day came when they
decided to set out to find homes
of their own.

"Remember to look out for the
Big Bad Wolf." Said their mother.

It wasn't long before they met
a man with a load of straw.

"I could build a very good house with that straw," said the first little pig and he bought the lot. He worked hard and by dinnertime, he had built himself a very snug little house.

Suddenly there was a knock at the door. It was the Big Bad Wolf!

"Little pig, little pig, let me come in!" called the wolf.

"No, no, by the hair on my chinny chin chin, I will not let you in!" said the first little pig.

"Then I'll huff and I'll puff and
I'll blow your house down!"
growled the wolf.

The Big, Bad Wolf took a deep breath.
He huffed and he puffed and he blew the house
down! The first little pig ran off as fast
as his trotters could carry him.

Meanwhile, the second and third
little pigs had walked on down the
winding road. Soon they met
a man with a load of sticks.

"I could make myself a very
good house with those sticks,"
said the second little pig.

He waved
goodbye to his
sister and before
long, he had built
a snug little house.

Suddenly there
came a knock at
the door. It was
the first little pig!

"Let me in!"
he cried. "The Big,
Bad Wolf is close behind me!"

"Little pigs, little pigs, let me come in!"

"No, no, by the hair on our chinny chin chins,"
replied the two little pigs, "we will not let
you in!"

"Then I'll huff and I'll puff and I'll blow your
house down!" The Big, Bad Wolf took a deep
breath and he huffed, and he puffed and he
blew the house down!

Meanwhile, the third little pig had met a man with a cart full of bricks and she had quickly built a lovely house.

Suddenly, there came a hammering at the door. "Let us in, let us in!" cried her brothers. "The Big, Bad Wolf is on his way!"

It wasn't long before they heard the wolf outside. "Little pigs, little pigs, let me come in!"

"No, no, by the hair on our chinny chin chins," chorused the three little pigs, "we will not let you in!"

"Then I'll huff and I'll puff and I'll blow your house down!" fumed the wolf.

He huffed and he puffed.
The brick house stood
strong and true. Now the
wolf was really angry.

"He's trying to climb down
the chimney!" whispered
the girl pig. "Help me with
this pot!"

The pigs dragged a huge pot on to the fire and
filled it with water. By the time the wolf had
squeezed himself down the chimney, the pot was
boiling and he dipped his tail in the hot water.

"Yeeeeeooowwww!" he yelled. That Big, Bad Wolf
shot straight up the chimney and off down the
road. He was never seen again, and the three
little pigs lived happily ever after.

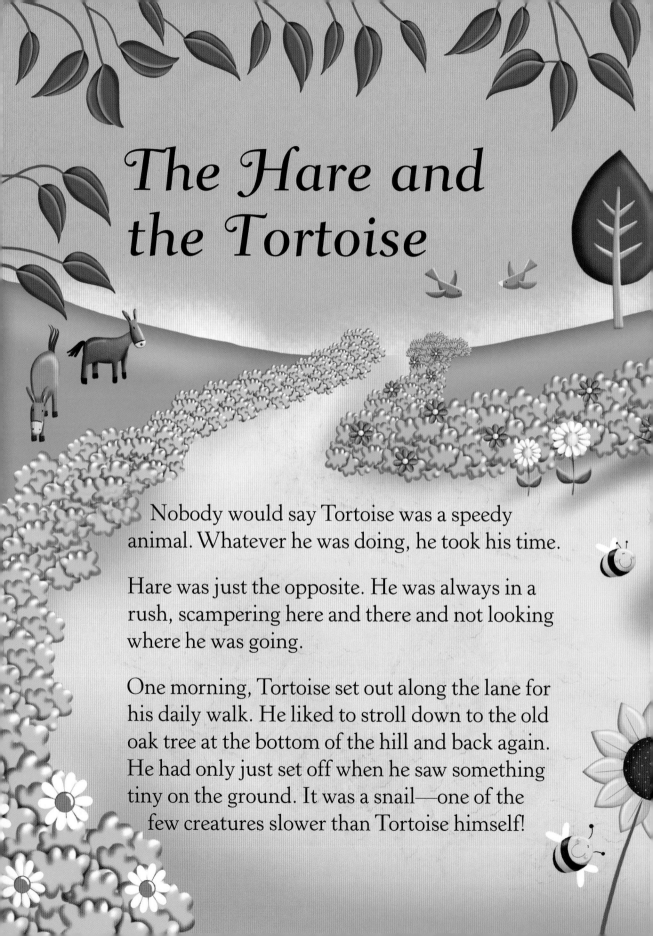

The Hare and the Tortoise

Nobody would say Tortoise was a speedy animal. Whatever he was doing, he took his time.

Hare was just the opposite. He was always in a rush, scampering here and there and not looking where he was going.

One morning, Tortoise set out along the lane for his daily walk. He liked to stroll down to the old oak tree at the bottom of the hill and back again. He had only just set off when he saw something tiny on the ground. It was a snail—one of the few creatures slower than Tortoise himself!

At that moment, Hare came hurtling up the hill. BUMP! Poor Tortoise spun right round in the road.

The surprise left Hare speechless for a moment, which gave Tortoise a chance to speak up.

"You really must be more careful, Hare," he said in his usual slow way. "You'll never get anywhere rushing around like you do."

Hare laughed, "I'll get further than you, old slowpoke," he chortled. "Are you going to the oak tree? I could be there and back before you got started."

"I don't think you could, you know," said Tortoise.

"That sounds like a challenge!" yelled Hare, bouncing about in the road now. "Let's have a race!"

"Fair enough," said Tortoise, slowly.

Off zoomed Hare. He was out of sight in seconds. Tortoise plodded on, just as he always did.

Meanwhile, Hare was dashing down the lane, so full of himself that he jumped and skipped as he went. By the time he reached the oak tree, he was out of breath.

"I'll just sit down here for a minute," said Hare to himself. "It will take all morning for Tortoise to get here. I've got plenty of time."

The sun was warm. Before long, Hare began to feel drowsy and soon he began to snore.

When Tortoise came slowly into view half an hour later, Hare was still asleep. Tortoise didn't say a word. He just kept walking.

It was lunchtime when Hare woke up and remembered the race. He jumped to his feet and shot off down the lane. There was no sign of Tortoise.

Hare ran faster than he had ever run before— that's pretty fast! He skidded to a stop outside Tortoise's house. To his horror, the door opened and the slow old creature appeared.

"Wah? Hah? How?" panted Hare.

"Slow and steady wins the race," said Tortoise, slowly and steadily. "Come on in."

The Little Red Hen

There was once a little red hen who lived with her friends on a farm. One day, she found some ears of wheat that had fallen from the farmer's truck. She didn't eat them right away, for as soon as she saw them, she had an idea.

"Who will help me plant this wheat?" she asked her friends.

"Well, I won't," said the cat.

"Nor will I," said the rat.

"I simply can't," said the pig.

"Then I'll do it myself,"
said the little red hen.
And she did.

The tiny grains of wheat
grew and grew into tall
stems with ripe ears of
wheat at the top.
The little red hen saw
that the wheat was
ready to be cut.

"Who will help me harvest
the wheat?" she asked.

 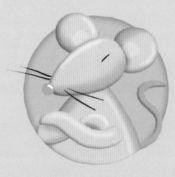 

"Well, I won't," said the cat.

"Nor will I," said the rat.

"I simply can't," said the pig.

"Then I'll do it myself," said the little red hen.
And she did.

"Who will help me take the
wheat to the mill to be ground into flour?"
asked the little red hen.

"Well, I won't," said the cat.

"Nor will I," said the rat.

"I simply can't," said the pig.

"Then I'll do it myself," said the little red hen.
And she did.

"Who will help me make some bread with this
flour?" she asked her friends.

"Well, I won't," said the cat.

"Nor will I," said the rat.

"I simply can't," said the pig.

"Then I'll do it myself," said the little red hen.
And she did.

Soon a wonderful smell came from the
farmhouse kitchen. The bread was ready!

"Who will help me to eat my delicious bread?"
called the little red hen.

"Well, I will!" said the cat.

"So will I!" said the rat.

"I simply can't wait!"
said the pig.

The little red hen
saw that the cat and
the rat and the pig were
not really friends at all.

"No," she said, "I think
I'll eat it myself."
And she did.

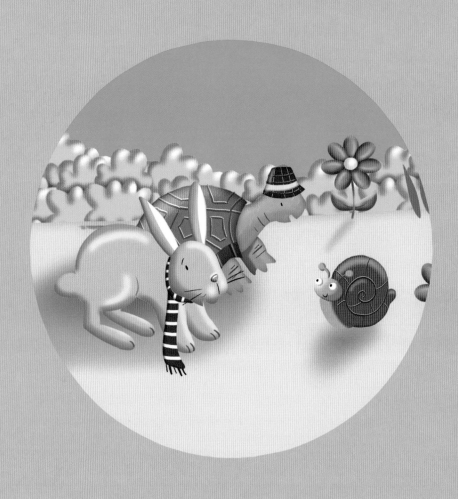

This edition published in 2012 by Arcturus Publishing Limited
26/27 Bickels Yard, 151–153 Bermondsey Street,
London SE1 3HA

ISBN: 978-1-84858-684-0
CH002332US
Supplier 15, Date 0412, Print run 1760

Printed in China